When Things Are Hard, Remember

To my parents, thank you for never giving up on me when things were hard.
Some things in life just take longer to sprout. And to my husband, Matt, and
my kids Katherine, Amber, and Makenna. Remember, when things are hard,
we'll always have each other. —J.R.

To my mum, brother, and sister. Times are hard, but our roots are stronger. —M.C.

26 25 24 23 22 21 20   1 2 3 4 5 6 7 8

Hardcover ISBN: 978-1-5064-6380-3
Ebook ISBN: 978-1-5064-6660-6

Library of Congress Cataloging-in-Publication Data
Names: Rowland, Joanna, author. | Calderón, Marcela, illustrator.
Title: When things are hard, remember / by Joanna Rowland ; illustrated by
   Marcela Calderón.
Description: Minneapolis, MN : Beaming Books, an imprint of 1517 Media,
   2020. | Audience: Ages 3-8. | Summary: Even as the world changes around
   her, a little girl has faith that circumstances will improve.
Identifiers: LCCN 2020005042 (print) | LCCN 2020005043 (ebook) | ISBN
   9781506463803 (hardcover) | ISBN 9781506466606 (ebook)
Subjects: CYAC: Faith--Fiction. | Hope--Fiction. | Change--Fiction. |
   Moving, Household--Fiction.
Classification: LCC PZ7.R7972 Wh 2020 (print) | LCC PZ7.R7972 (ebook) |
   DDC [E]--dc23
LC record available at https://lccn.loc.gov/2020005042
LC ebook record available at https://lccn.loc.gov/20200050

VN0004589; 9781506463803; NOV2020

Beaming Books
510 Marquette Avenue
Minneapolis, MN 55402
Beamingbooks.com

When Things Are Hard, Remember

by Joanna Rowland

illustrated by Marcela Calderón

beaming ☀ books

MINNEAPOLIS

You're small,
protected, and loved.

Shelter keeps you safe and warm,
surrounded by others.

But then something changes,
and it's time to move away.

You're scared and lonely. And that's okay.

On days when your faith is shaken,
remember the tree
that loses all its leaves,

the animals hibernating beneath the snow,
the baby turtle getting ready to hatch.

Faith is hoping—through winter's cold, amid crunching snow and blowing wind—that everything will be all right.

Faith is believing—
even when things are hard,
on an unknown journey,
when you aren't sure what will happen next—
that you will be taken care of.

In time, you'll find that even though it's raining, and darkness surrounds you,

you'll break out of your shell
and begin to settle roots.

When your roots take hold, you'll begin to sprout
and feel the warmth of the sun again.

Soon you'll see
you were always cared for,
even during your hardest time.

And you'll be like the tree with new blooms,
the animals who awoke to spring's promise,
the turtle that found its way to the water's edge.

And you'll have faith for the next time
things are hard—faith that something new,
something beautiful will sprout . . .

just like you!

About the Author and Illustrator

JOANNA ROWLAND is the author of the award-winning picture book *The Memory Box: A Book About Grief.* She writes comforting books that offer support and encouragement to children during difficult times. Joanna lives in Sacramento, California.

MARCELA CALDERÓN is a children's book illustrator who grew up in Argentina, surrounded by streams, trees, nature, and pets that were her drawing inspirations.